# Over the Moon!

# Crabtree Publishing Company
www.crabtreebooks.com
1-800-387-7650

PMB 16A, 350 Fifth Ave.
Suite 3308,
New York, NY

616 Welland Ave.
St. Catharines, ON
L2M 5V6

Published by Crabtree Publishing in 2010

**Series Editor:** Jackie Hamley
**Editor:** Reagan Miller
**Series Advisor:** Dr. Hilary Minns
**Series Designer:** Peter Scoulding
**Editorial Director:** Kathy Middleton

Text © Hilary Robinson 2006
Illustration © Jane Abbott 2006

The rights of the author and the illustrator
of this Work have been asserted.

For Molly, Zachary
and India with love – J.A.

For Lucas – H.R.

First published in 2006
by Franklin Watts
(A division of Hachette
Children's Books)

P

**Library and Archives Canada
Cataloguing in Publication**

Robinson, Hilary, 1962-
        Over the moon! / Hilary Robinson ; illustrated
by Jane Abbott.

(Tadpoles)
ISBN 978-0-7787-3868-8 (bound).--
ISBN 978-0-7787-3899-2 (pbk.)

    1. Readers (Primary).  I. Abbott, Jane (Jane D.)  .
II. Title.  III. Series: Tadpoles (St. Catharines, Ont.)

PE1117.T33 2009d        428.6        C2009-903986-9

**Library of Congress
Cataloging-in-Publication Data**

**Available at Library of Congress**

# Over the Moon!

by Hilary Robinson

Illustrated by Jane Abbott

## Crabtree Publishing Company

www.crabtreebooks.com

## Hilary Robinson

"I have always liked watching the magical night sky, and I would love to be the first author to jump over the moon!"

## Jane Abbott

"The nursery rhyme that this story comes from is one of my children's favorites. I really like the ending in this story!"

The cow and the cat
looked up at the Moon,
shining high in the sky.

"Look!" said the cat.
"Let's jump over that!"

6

"Oh yes!" said the cow.
"Let's try!"

The little dog laughed
at the cat and the cow.

They jumped ...

... but they could not jump high!

"Look!" said the cat.
"By the dish and
the spoon,

the Moon has
dropped out
of the sky!"

Then all that night
they sang out a tune.

"Tonight is the night that the cow and the cat ...

"...ran and jumped over the Moon!"

# Notes for adults

**TADPOLES** are structured to provide support for early readers. The stories m also be used by adults for sharing with young children.

Starting to read alone can be daunting. **TADPOLES** help by providing visual support and repeating high frequency words and phrases. These books will b develop confidence and encourage reading and rereading for pleasure.

**If you are reading this book with a child, here are a few suggestions:**

1. Make reading fun! Choose a time to read when you and the child are relaxed and have time to share the story.
2. Talk about the story before you start reading. Look at the cover and the blurb. What might the story be about? Why might the child like it?
3. Encourage the child to reread the story, and to retell the story in their own words, using the illustrations to remind them what has happened.
4. Discuss the story and see if the child can relate it to their own experiences, or perhaps compare it to another story they know.
5. Give praise! Children learn best in a positive environment.

**If you enjoyed this book, why not try another TADPOLES story?**

**At the End of the Garden**
9780778738503 RLB
9780778738817 PB

**Bad Luck, Lucy!**
9780778738510 RLB
9780778738824 PB

**Ben and the Big Balloon**
9780778738602 RLB
9780778738916 PB

**Crabby Gabby**
9780778738527 RLB
9780778738831 PB

**Dad's Cake**
9780778738657 RLB
9780778738961 PB

**Dad's Van**
9780778738664 RLB
9780778738978 PB

**The Dinosaur Next Door**
9780778738732 RLB
9780778739043 PB

**Five Teddy Bears**
9780778738534 RLB
9780778738848 PB

**I'm Taller Than You!**
9780778738541 RLB
9780778738855 PB

**Leo's New Pet**
9780778738558 RLB
9780778738862 PB

**Little Troll**
9780778738565 RLB
9780778738879 PB

**Mop Top**
9780778738572 RLB
9780778738886 PB

**My Auntie Susan**
9780778738589 RLB
9780778738893 PB

**My Big, New Bed**
9780778738596 RLB
9780778738909 PB

**Night, Night**
9780778738671 RLB
9780778738985 PB

**Over the Moon!**
9780778738688 RLB
9780778738992 PB

**Pirate Pete**
9780778738619 RLB
9780778738923 PB

**Rooster's Alarm**
9780778738749 RLB
9780778739050 PB

**Runny Honey**
9780778738626 RLB
9780778738930 PB

**The Sad Princess**
9780778738725 RLB
9780778739036 PB

**Sammy's Secret**
9780778738633 RLB
9780778738947 PB

**Sam's Sunflower**
9780778738640 RLB
9780778738954 PB

**Tag!**
9780778738695 RLB
9780778739005 PB

**Ted's Party Bus**
9780778738701 RLB
9780778739012 PB

**Tortoise Races Home**
9780778738718 RLB
9780778739029 PB